RUNAWAYS

David Belbin was born in Sheffield, later living in Leicester, Merseyside and Lancashire. He went to university in Nottingham, where he has stayed ever since. He has worked as a street sweeper, grass cutter, conservation ranger, drystone waller, Credit Union officer and English teacher. He now makes a living by writing novels and short stories for young people of all ages. His books include *The Beat*, a series about young police officers, *The Foggiest*, *Love Lessons* and *Haunting Time*, a collection of short stories.

SURFERS

David Belbin

PUFFIN BOOKS

For Declan and Conor

PUFFIN BOOKS

Published by the Penguin Group
Penguin Books Ltd, 27 Wrights Lane, London W8 5TZ, England
Penguin Putnam Inc., 375 Hudson Street, New York, New York 10014, USA
Penguin Books Australia Ltd, Ringwood, Victoria, Australia
Penguin Books Canada Ltd, 10 Alcorn Avenue, Toronto, Ontario, Canada M4V 3B2
Penguin Books (NZ) Ltd, Private Bag 102902, NSMC, Auckland, New Zealand

On the World Wide Web at: www.penguin.com

Penguin Books Ltd, Registered Offices: Harmondsworth, Middlesex, England

First published 2000
1 3 5 7 9 10 8 6 4 2

Set in Bembo

Made and printed in England by Clays Ltd, St Ives plc

British Library Cataloguing in Publication Data
A CIP catalogue record for this book is available from the British Library

ISBN 0–141–30289–5

Contents

Chapter One
Running Late

JACK HAD ONLY two minutes to make his train. Heart pumping, he dragged his heavy suitcase up two flights of steps. Next, he had to cross a bridge. Finally, he went down more steps and on to the platform. There was no train.

Maybe it was late. Yet hardly anybody else stood on the cold platform. There was a girl about his age. She wore sunglasses, even though the day was overcast. A soldier sat on a bench smoking. An old lady was on the other bench, looking for something in her carpet bag. None of them seemed concerned. They were probably waiting for a different train.

Jack couldn't believe it. There were only two trains a day to Clanark. The other one had gone hours ago. The only way to reach his father tonight would be if Dad came to collect him. But his dad was a hundred miles away and didn't even know that Jack was coming.

Jack looked at the station clock which said one minute past four. The train was meant to leave at three fifty-eight. What was he going to do? All he had on him was a fiver and some change for the phone. Dad wouldn't be home yet. There was no point in ringing him.

'Are you all right, young man?' Someone was tapping Jack on the shoulder with an umbrella. It was a portly, balding gentleman with mischievous eyes. Jack half expected him to be a policeman, but he wasn't.

'I ... I missed my train,' Jack told him. 'I need to find a phone.'

'You'll find one further down the platform, just beyond the Gents.'

'Thanks very much.'

As Jack dragged his bag along the platform, there was an announcement over the tannoy.

'The next train to arrive at platform five will be the delayed fifteen fifty-eight service to Bragoon via Carlisle. The train will now depart at sixteen-o-seven. We apologize for the delay which was due to driver illness.'

The Bragoon train was the one which went to Clanark. Everything was all right! Jack breathed a huge sigh of relief. He even had time to phone Dad. Jack wasn't sure that he had enough money for a taxi from Clanark station. Maybe, if he left a message on the machine, Dad would get it in time to come and collect him. Jack walked over to the girl in the dark glasses.

'Could you watch my bag for me?' he asked, in a hurry. 'I need to make a phone call. I'll only be a minute.'

Jack sprinted to the phone box without waiting for an answer. He dialled the number. His father's warm voice invited him to leave a message after the tone.

'Hi, Dad, it's me. I'm coming to see you a couple of weeks early. I'll be at

Clanark station at five fourteen. No, more like twenty-five past because the train's been delayed. I'll get a bus or a taxi or something if you don't turn up.'

The pips went. There was no time for further explanation. Jack hurried back to the girl in the sunglasses who was guarding his suitcase.

'Thanks,' he said.

'Is your bag still there?' she asked.

'Of course,' Jack replied, confused. 'Right here. Can't you see?'

'No,' she told him. 'I'm blind.'

Chapter Two

Strangers on a Train

SHE WASN'T KIDDING. Jack had been too hyped up to notice her stick. He apologized, then asked the obvious question.

'You're blind and you're travelling alone?'

'Why not?' she asked him. 'My dad put me on the train and my mum's meeting me off it. I get a guide dog next year, but I can do without one. All I need is a guard or someone to

help me change trains here. You'll
do!'

They introduced themselves. Her
name was Hannah.

'I'm on my way to see my dad,' Jack
explained.

Hannah smiled knowingly. 'Are your
parents divorced?'

'Yeah,' Jack told her in a weary voice.
'Two years.'

'Mine broke up four years ago,'
Hannah told him. 'You get used to it.'

'I guess.'

'Do you go to school in Scotland?'
she asked.

'No. England. Near Preston.'

'Don't English schools still have ten
days before the end of term?'

'Yes,' Jack said. 'They do.'

He changed the subject rapidly.

'Where does your mum live?'

'The end of the line,' Hannah told him. 'Bragoon. The train's coming now. I can hear it.'

Moments later, the train rolled into the station. Its engine clanked and groaned. The train was dirty and old. As it pulled to a stop, there was another announcement.

'The train arriving at platform five is the delayed fifteen fifty-eight to Bragoon. Passengers travelling beyond Carlisle are asked to travel in the first carriage only.'

Jack helped Hannah into the crowded first carriage. He'd hoped to sit with her, but she had a reserved seat and the ones around her were taken. The nearest empty seat was on the other side of the aisle.

'Is this free?'

It was the old lady who Jack had seen earlier. She took the seat nearest the aisle, stopping Jack from talking to Hannah. Maybe it was just as well. He didn't want to answer any more awkward questions about why he was travelling.

The noisy train set off. The old lady quickly fell asleep. Jack got out a puzzle magazine. He'd been working his way through it without much success. He had so much on his mind that it was hard to concentrate.

When Jack got stuck on his crossword, he looked around. There were two men in the seat in front of him. One was balding and was wearing some kind of uniform beneath his overcoat. The other had very short hair.

That was all Jack could see. The two men didn't speak to each other and Jack couldn't tell whether they were together or not.

To his right was Hannah and a young man who looked like a student. Behind them was the soldier – he had just got up and was making his way down the carriage. He was probably going to the buffet car, which was in a different carriage. Hannah got out a personal stereo and put on the headphones.

After a few minutes, the ticket collector came by. He woke the old lady.

When the man had checked their tickets, the old lady turned to Jack. 'Would you like a sweet?' she asked, reaching into a pocket of her cardigan. She held out a paper bag full of pink and white sweets, shaped like mussels. They smelt funny.

'What are they?' he asked.

'Sugared almonds.'

'No, thanks. I'm allergic to some nuts.'

'Oh dear,' the old lady said. 'You ought to be very careful, then.'

'I am.'

To Jack's surprise, the old lady didn't ask him any more questions. Elderly people often quizzed you about your interests, where you were going, school and stuff like that. But this old lady seemed too tense to talk. Maybe she was naturally grumpy.

Jack got through his last bar of chocolate and a copy of *Shoot* before the train reached Carlisle. The old lady didn't leave her seat once, not even to visit the toilet. Eventually, Jack needed to go. On the way back to his seat, he stopped to talk to Hannah. The student had left, so the seat next to her was free. He tapped Hannah on the shoulder.

'Hello again,' Jack said. 'It's me. Been listening to anything interesting?'

'A story called *The Thirty-nine Steps*,' Hannah said, with a smile. 'Though it's hard to hear properly over the engine. What have you been up to?'

'Reading and doing some puzzles.'

'Get them all right?' she asked.

'Nearly. There were a few crossword answers I couldn't get.'

'Maybe I could help,' Hannah said.

'Er ...'

Hannah frowned. 'Just because I'm blind, it doesn't mean that I can't do crosswords. All you have to do is read the clues to me.'

Jack got his magazine, then sat down next to her. Hannah immediately got two of the answers he'd missed.

'This one's been really bugging me: "You're dead, son! So you won't get out of here in a hurry (6)." What on earth could that mean?'

'Maybe it's an anagram,' Hannah said. 'You know, where you rearrange the letters in a word to make another word. Like changing "boy" into "yob".'

'I know what an anagram is,' Jack said. 'But there are too many letters in the clue to make a six-letter word.'

'The trick is to know which bit of the clue is the anagram.'

Hannah stared out of the window, thinking.

'What's another way of saying that somebody's dead? Rest in peace. RIP.'

'So?' Jack said. 'What's your point?'

Hannah grinned. 'Rearrange "RIP" and add "son". You make a place that's very hard to get out of.'

'Of course!' Jack yelled, very impressed. 'Prison!'

The uniformed man sitting at the front of the carriage turned round and gave Jack a funny look.

'Sorry,' Jack said to him. 'I didn't mean to disturb you.'

The man turned back without saying anything.

'Let's see if we can get another one,' Hannah said, as the train rolled into Carlisle.

They were busy with the crossword when the train stopped. Only one newcomer got into their carriage – a young woman in her early twenties.

She had short hair and a stud through her nose. She tried to sit next to the old lady.

'I'm sorry,' the old lady said. 'This is that young man's seat.'

'It doesn't matter,' Jack said, but the woman had already moved into one of the empty seats behind them. Another young woman got on. She had blonde hair and wore the red railway uniform. She was pushing a trolley full of hot drinks.

'Complimentary tea and coffee from Scottish Railways,' she announced. 'We apologize for the short delay.'

Everybody took one except for Hannah and Jack. As the woman disappeared into the front of the train, the old lady opposite began to rummage in her carpet bag. Then she got up out of her seat. Suddenly she was all smiles.

'Here,' she said to Jack and Hannah, proffering a paper bag. 'You'll like these. Special toffee from Cornwall. You must have a piece.'

'Thanks,' Jack said, though he didn't like toffee much. It made his teeth feel all sticky. Politely, he took one.

'You have one too, dear,' the lady said to Hannah.

'I'm fine, thank you. I had lots of toffee earlier.'

'No, dear, you must try these. You've never had toffee as nice as this. Please, I insist.'

Hannah took one. Reluctantly, she put the toffee in her mouth. The old lady didn't go back to her seat, but walked to the end of the carriage.

Presumably she was going to use the toilet.

'These toffees taste funny,' Hannah whispered to Jack, 'mildewed.'

Jack didn't notice anything odd about the taste. However, Hannah sounded very certain. Maybe there was something wrong with the toffee. Jack spat his out into his hand. Then he told Hannah what he'd done and she did the same.

'Here', she said and held out a tissue on which was placed her uneaten toffee. Jack put his sweet into it.

Just then there was an announcement. 'This train will continue on the branch line to Bragoon very shortly.'

The soldier came back into the carriage, a can of beer in his hand. Hannah touched Jack's shoulder.

Gently, she pulled him closer to her.

'So tell me,' she whispered, 'why have you run away from home?'

Chapter Three
Runaway

JACK WAS THROWN by Hannah's question.

'What makes you think ... ?' he began to ask.

'I often feel like running away myself,' Hannah told him. 'Only, being the way I am, I wouldn't get very far. Was it a row or something more serious?'

Jack didn't answer at first. He had to decide whether to trust her.

'It wasn't all that serious,' he mumbled eventually.

'Are you going to tell me what happened?' Hannah asked. 'I don't mean to pry. Only tell me if you want to.'

'I guess it's all right,' Jack said. 'I'm going to have to tell Dad anyhow. The thing is, I fell out with Steve.'

'Who's Steve?'

'My mum's new husband. She married him last year. Steve's a plumber. She met him when he came to fix the washing machine. He was nice at first. Said he didn't want to take Dad's place, but we could be mates. He used to take me to the pictures and the football. But he stopped trying after they got married. Then, back in March, Mum had a new baby.'

He hesitated.

'And you ceased to exist?' Hannah suggested.

'Except when we're having rows. These days, it's total war. Last night, Steve accused me of stealing some money from his wallet. I've never stolen anything in my life! But Mum took his side. She said ... are you all right?'

Hannah was slumping against his shoulder.

'I'm sorry,' she murmured. 'I suddenly feel very tired.'

'I didn't mean to bore you.'

'It's not that,' she muttered. 'I understand what you're ... It's just ...'

Her glasses slipped and Jack saw that her eyes were closed. He found he felt tired himself, but fought the sensation. The toffees, he thought ... But he'd barely sucked his before spitting it out ... *There was something wrong with the toffees.*

Then he fell asleep.

Jack slept heavily. He dreamt of going past his station and finding himself in an army camp. A sergeant told him off for not making his bed properly ...

Suddenly, he awoke with a jolt. He was slumped across Hannah who was still asleep. Jack looked around. The two men sitting together at the front of the carriage seemed to be asleep too. The little old lady who had given him the toffee was nowhere to be seen.

The only people awake were the blonde woman who'd served the drinks and the soldier. He sat behind Hannah, drinking his beer.

The train clickety-clacked along the branch line. Jack looked out of the window and saw the shadows of the dark hills through the relentless rain.

Then he looked for the rest of the train. It wasn't there. Of course, the other carriages had been uncoupled at Carlisle. They weren't needed for the handful of people going beyond.

Suddenly, Jack needed the loo. He walked to the back of the carriage. The only toilet was engaged. He wondered who else was still on the train. Jack waited a couple of minutes. There was no sound from within the toilet. No one came out. He started back to his seat. As Jack passed him, the soldier caught his eye.

'Someone's been in there since Carlisle,' he said.

Jack looked at his watch. They had left Carlisle over half an hour ago.

'Maybe nobody's inside,' he said. 'Maybe the lock's broken.'

'We could see,' the soldier said. 'I need to go myself.'

They went to the door and knocked. There was no reply.

'Hello,' Jack called. 'Do you need any help?'

No reply. The soldier shook the handle. 'Definitely locked on the inside.'

Jack began to worry. 'There was this old lady,' he said, 'sitting next to me. She's not there now, so maybe she's in here.'

'I'm going to try and force it!' the soldier said.

He rammed his shoulder against the door. It shook, but didn't budge. They were joined by the young blonde woman.

'Kicking it might be better,' she said.

The three of them took turns at

kicking the door. Soon it was dented, but it still didn't open. They stopped for a rest.

'Are you sure there's someone in there?' the blonde woman asked.

'Pretty sure,' Jack said. 'Do you remember the old lady who was sitting next to me?'

'I didn't see any old lady,' the young woman said.

'Me neither,' the soldier said. 'She wasn't in the carriage when I came back from the buffet car.'

'Then she must be in here,' Jack told them. 'I'll go and see if her stuff's still there.'

He went back to her seat. The old lady's carpet bag wasn't there. Maybe she'd taken it to the toilet with her. He looked on the rack above, where his suitcase was. There was nothing near it, nothing that could belong to the old lady. Maybe she'd left the train.

But the old lady had stayed on the train in Carlisle for several minutes. Why would she have done that if she was going to get off? It made no sense. But Jack still felt groggy and wasn't thinking straight. How many other people should still be in the carriage? Six? There were only four people sitting down. Five, if you counted the blonde woman.

'The old lady must be in there!' he told the soldier urgently. 'She might be sick!'

'All right,' the soldier said. 'Calm down. We'll get it open somehow. And if we don't succeed, the first stop isn't far off. We can get help there.'

He knocked on the door one more time. 'Is anybody in there? Wake up!'

Then he reached into his army jacket and pulled out a knife.

'I might be able to break the lock,' he said, pointing it at the door.

But before he could have a go at it, they heard the bolt slide across. The door opened slowly and there was the young woman with the short hair and the stud through her nose. Jack had forgotten all about her.

'I fell asleep,' she mumbled.

Then she saw the soldier with the knife in his hand and fainted.

Chapter Four
Sleepers

JACK HELPED THE soldier carry the woman back to her seat.

'What's going on?' the soldier asked. 'The whole carriage seems to be asleep.'

Jack decided to trust him. 'I think everybody's been given a sleeping drug. You missed it because you were in the buffet car until just before we left Carlisle.'

The soldier didn't believe him. 'Why would people take a sleeping pill?'

Jack explained about the free tea and coffee. Then he mentioned the old lady's toffee and how he had hardly started his.

'A boy who doesn't like toffee?' the soldier said, surprised. 'This gets stranger and stranger. Are you sure you didn't dream up this little old lady who vanished?'

'Why don't we ask the other people?' Jack said. 'I'll prove that she was here.'

They went to the young blonde woman first.

'I haven't seen any old ladies,' she said to the soldier, 'with toffees or otherwise. And if this is your idea of a chat-up line ...'

'No, no,' the soldier said, moving rapidly on. 'It's just that this kid is worried about the woman who was sitting next to him, that's all.'

Jack hated being called a 'kid', but he followed the soldier along the carriage. The young woman from the toilet had gone back into a deep sleep, so she was no help. Hannah was still asleep too. Jack shook her awake.

'What is it?' she said. 'Who is it?'

'Jack. Remember? We were doing the crossword. I'm worried about the old lady who was sitting next to me. The one who gave us the toffees.'

'She couldn't have seen her,' the soldier interrupted. 'We're wasting our time. Come on, let's try these guys at the front.'

'I'll be back in a minute,' Jack promised Hannah. He followed the soldier. He hadn't seen these men's faces before. As far as he knew, they hadn't moved since he'd got on the train. Now he saw that they were both fast asleep.

'Excuse me.'

The soldier poked the ribs of the younger man, who had short, fair hair. His eyes flicked open. He looked alert, as though he hadn't been asleep at all, but faking.

'Have you seen …' the soldier began.

The young man shushed him. 'My mate's trying to get some kip.'

The soldier whispered, 'All we want to know is whether you've seen an old lady. She was sitting in the seat behind you.'

'Old lady? Can't say I did. Sorry.'

The young man closed his eyes, dismissing them.

'Looks like you made her up, mate,'

the soldier said, sitting down in Jack's old seat. 'Bit of a dreamer, are you?'

Jack frowned. He sat down in the old lady's seat, ignoring Hannah, who had gone back to sleep. He looked out of the window. Grey rain slashed the dark countryside. Hopefully he would be with Dad soon. Then the old lady wouldn't matter.

But she *did* matter. Jack looked beneath his seat to see if the old lady had left anything behind, anything at all. But there were no half-sucked sugar almonds, no paper bags or bits of knitting. Maybe he *had* imagined her.

Mum said that Jack was always imagining things, like the bad feeling between him and his stepfather. But this was more than a feeling. He had seen her. So why was everybody pretending that the old lady had never been on the train? And where had she gone?

Slowly, Hannah became aware of the sound of the train. Its rapid rumble was a little unusual, she thought. Why was she so sleepy? She remembered Jack asking about the old lady. He'd said he'd return, but she'd gone back to sleep. Suddenly, she heard Jack's voice.

'Are you awake again?'

'Yes,' Hannah told him. 'I don't know why I'm so tired. Did you say that the old lady's gone?'

'Yes,' Jack whispered. 'And it's weird. Everybody on the train says they didn't see her.'

'I did,' Hannah said.

'But …' Jack sounded embarrassed.

'Sorry,' Hannah said. 'Blind people

say "see" when they mean "heard" or "been with". It's just a manner of speaking. Why do you think people are lying about the old lady?'

'I wish I knew,' Jack said.

'There's probably some simple explanation,' Hannah offered. 'Like there's probably a simple explanation for why you've run away from home. Tell me again. I fell asleep when you were explaining before.'

Jack finished telling her the story in as few words as he could manage, ending with the row he'd had with Steve the night before.

'So I sneaked a suitcase out of the cupboard late last night and packed for the whole summer. This morning, before Mum or Steve got up, I hid my suitcase beneath my bed. I rushed home from school, picked up the case and got a taxi to the station.'

'Won't your mum be back from work by now?'

Jack looked at his watch. It was nearly five.

'Yes,' he said. 'But I left her a note explaining. Anyway, I'll ring her when I get to Dad's.'

'We still haven't worked out why everyone fell asleep,' Hannah said, after a long pause.

'I think it was the sweets,' Jack told her. 'I think there was some kind of knockout drop in the toffee,' he explained.

'All right,' Hannah said. 'Maybe. But what about the other people?'

'They got free tea and coffee at Carlisle.'

'Who from?' Hannah asked.

'The blonde woman,' Jack whispered. 'She's wearing a railway uniform. And she's still awake.'

'Let me see if I've got this straight,' said Hannah. 'The two men in the front seats and the woman with the stud through her nose are asleep. We're awake. So is the soldier and the blonde woman. But the old lady is missing.'

'Yes,' Jack said. 'What do you think?'

'It's probably coincidence,' Hannah said. 'People fall asleep on trains all the time.'

'Not this heavily. We nearly had to break the toilet door down before the woman in there woke up. Also, why did the bloke in front lie about seeing the old lady?'

'Maybe he didn't notice her,' Hannah replied, but it got her thinking.

'There's something really strange going on,' Jack said. 'Hey!'

'What is it?' Hannah asked.

'We're passing Dumgellen station. I'm sure the train was meant to stop here.'

Hannah shrugged. 'Sounds like you're wrong.'

'What's wrong, son?' the soldier asked.

Jack told him.

'Trains can't stop at every little station,' the soldier said.

'We think there's something funny going on,' Hannah told him.

The soldier laughed. 'You haven't been hallucinating little old ladies too, have you?'

37

Hannah snarled. She hated it when adults condescended to her. 'You weren't here,' she said. 'How can you know about the old lady?'

'And you can't see,' the soldier said. 'So how can you know?'

There was no satisfactory answer to that. Still, Jack defended her.

'She heard her. We both took a toffee.'

'Didn't anybody tell you not to take sweets from strangers?' the soldier said.

'We didn't finish them,' Hannah pointed out. She reached into her pocket and found the tissue from earlier. 'Take this off me, Jack. Show him.'

Jack took the tissue and opened it out for the soldier.

'Two sticky toffees,' he said. 'What does that prove?'

Neither Jack nor Hannah answered. The soldier walked back down the aisle. Hannah heard him talking to the young woman, but couldn't make out their conversation.

'We're nearly at my station,' Jack said.

'Oh,' Hannah said. She was worried now. When Jack got off, she would be stuck with three sleeping people, plus the soldier and the blonde.

'There's something really wrong here,' she told Jack. 'When you get off, maybe you should go to the police.'

'I'll tell my dad,' Jack said. 'If he thinks I should, then …'

'No,' Hannah insisted, 'you should call them straight away, even if your dad isn't there. I'm sure that old woman tried to drug us!'

'Maybe it was an accident,' Jack

suggested. 'Maybe there was something wrong with the toffees, but she didn't know about it.'

'I don't think so,' said Hannah. 'Now I think back, she sounded too friendly. A bit twitchy. You know what I mean? I'm sure she was up to something.'

'You're right,' Jack said. 'When I get off, I'll call the police.'

Jack's stop, Clanark, was coming up. The two men in front still slept. Jack reached up to get his case. The luggage rack was a bit high for him, but anyone who could have helped was either asleep or occupied.

Jack got hold of the suitcase handle and inched it towards him. They must be nearly at Clanark by now. The train was going faster than it had been earlier. Jack tried to keep his balance as he pulled the suitcase out.

The train gave a sudden lurch to the left. The suitcase shook free of Jack's hand. He thought for a moment that it was going to hit him. Jack stepped back, holding out his arms to try and catch it. But the suitcase slipped forward, banging into the heads of the sleeping men in front. Jack grabbed at it, pulling the case back on to the vacant seats behind them.

'I'm sorry!' he said. 'I'm so sorry.'

The man on the right twisted his hand round to feel the side of his head. The other man did nothing. Nothing at all.

'I'm so sorry,' Jack repeated.

'Forget it,' the short-haired young man mumbled and closed his eyes.

He seemed to have gone back to

sleep. His older companion hadn't woken, even though he got the harder knock. Jack thought he saw a thin line of blood on the man's temple.

'Are you sure he's all right?' Jack asked the short-haired man, who didn't reply.

There was no time to pursue the question. Jack dragged his suitcase towards the door. His station would soon be in sight. Why wasn't the train slowing down?

Hannah called to Jack. 'Where are we?'

'We're just coming into Clanark,' he told her, pulling his suitcase along the aisle and sitting beside her.

'You'll go to the police?' Hannah asked, in an urgent voice.

'I will,' he said. 'But ...'

'You don't think they'll believe you?'

'Maybe not.' Jack looked out of the window at the countryside thundering by. He felt worried about Hannah.

'Would you give me your phone number?' he said. 'I'd like to ring you tonight, make sure that the rest of the journey worked out all right.'

'OK,' she said. 'But I've got a funny feeling ...'

Jack took out his pen. Hannah felt in her pocket. She pulled out the two toffees.

'Why don't you take these to the police?'

'Good idea,' Jack said. 'They can get them analysed. Now, quick, your phone number!'

She told him, adding, 'I've got a mobile number too.'

Jack wrote it down.

'I wish I was getting off with you,' she said.

'So do I. I'd better get to the door.'

Jack finished dragging his suitcase to the end of the carriage. The young blonde woman gave him a funny look as he passed her. The woman with the stud through her nose was still asleep. Jack wondered if he'd ever see Hannah again. He wasn't that keen on girls as a rule, but he liked Hannah and he was worried about her.

Then Clanark station came into view. Jack pulled the window down, ready to open the door. Rain came in. There was one person standing on the tiny platform. He was holding a blue umbrella and wearing a familiar green raincoat. Jack had never felt more relieved to see his father.

But something wasn't right. The train wasn't slowing down. Jack stood at the door, staring through the window, his heart beating furiously. The train kept going. Jack could see his father's confused face.

'No!' Jack shouted, as the train passed through Clanark station at high speed. But the word was lost in the noise of the engine. Jack's dad only caught a glimpse of his son waving frantically through the open window. Something was wrong, Jack decided, really wrong. On the platform, a man in uniform frantically blew a whistle.

The train was out of control.

Chapter Five
Runaway Train

'ARE YOU ALL right, son?' the soldier asked, seeing Jack dragging his suitcase back up the carriage.

'No,' Jack said, trying not to sound too upset. 'The train didn't stop.'

The soldier got up and joined Jack in the passageway. 'Are you sure that it was meant to stop there?'

'Certain.'

'I'm beginning to think you're right. There's something funny going on here,' the soldier said. He called to the young blonde woman. 'Where are you getting off?'

'End of the line,' she said. 'Bragoon. I've finished work for the day.'

'Do you know how many times the train's meant to stop?' the soldier asked.

The young woman shrugged. 'I thought that this was a direct train. As far as I'm aware, it doesn't stop at all.'

'There's your explanation,' the soldier told Jack. 'Sounds like your dad got mixed up about the timetable. Easy mistake to make. I didn't know that there were any non-stop trains myself. Don't worry, when we get to Bragoon there's bound to be a slow train that'll take you back to Clanark.'

'I suppose,' Jack said. He sat down,

angry with himself for not checking the train times properly. The earlier announcement had only listed the names of the stations up to Carlisle. Otherwise, Jack might have realized that this train didn't stop at Clanark.

What should he do? Jack would have to ring his dad when he got to Bragoon to sort out the situation. It wasn't such a big deal. Still, Jack felt awful. Dad was bound to be angry that he had wasted his time. He'd probably be angry with him for running away as well. Everything about this journey was going wrong. Except for meeting Hannah. She spoke to him now.

'Does your dad have a mobile phone?'

Jack shook his head.

'I was going to say that you could use

my phone to call him, work out what to do.'

'Thanks,' Jack said. 'That's nice of you. Maybe I should give him time to get home, then call him there.'

'All right,' Hannah said. 'But shall I tell you something?'

'What?'

'I'm really glad that you're still on board. This train is creepy. Tell me, what's going on? Has anyone woken up?'

'Doesn't look like it,' Jack said. 'The soldier's still chatting up the blonde woman three seats behind you. That's all.'

He looked out of the window. The train was going awfully fast. The engine noise was louder than ever. The train seemed to shake and shudder as it juddered along the line. The soldier, he saw now, was beginning to look worried. He rejoined Jack and Hannah.

'You know, I've been using this train on every leave for the last year,' he said. 'I've never known one which doesn't stop at a dozen stations on the way.' He looked at his watch. 'Bencrach is any minute now.'

The two of them got up and looked out of the window. There was Bencrach station, but the train still showed no sign of slowing down. A stationmaster was on the platform, waving a yellow flag. If anything, the train seemed to speed up. They hurtled through the station.

'*Now* do you believe me?' Jack said. 'We've got to do something! The train's out of control.'

'Whatever we do,' the soldier said, 'we'd better do it in a hurry. We're on a single track now. There's a big junction coming up and we just went through a red light. That means there's another train coming. And we're going to crash into it!'

'We have to pull the communication cord!' Hannah said.

'You're right,' Jack said. Before the soldier could object, Jack jumped on to an empty seat. With his fist, he hit the glass covering the cord. It didn't break.

'Let me have a go,' the soldier said, pulling out his sheath knife.

Suddenly, the train gave an enormous shudder.

'There's no need,' Jack said, sitting down. 'We're stopping.'

The train braked sharply.

'I think we should get off while we have the chance,' Hannah said. 'Would you give me a hand?'

'Sure,' Jack replied.

'Where's that blonde gone?' the soldier asked, as they guided Hannah down the aisle.

'There she is.' Jack pointed out of the window.

The young woman was running along the railway track outside.

'Hold on,' the soldier said. 'She's doing something with the points!'

'What?' Hannah asked.

'Can't tell,' the soldier said. 'Look, I think I'd better go and have a word with the driver. Wait there.'

Reluctantly, Jack and Hannah let the soldier go. Jack stared out of the window.

'I think she's moved the points,' he told Hannah. 'That means we won't hit the train coming the other way. But there's a junction ahead. I reckon we're not heading to Bragoon any more. Hold on, she's coming back.'

The blonde woman was running back to the train. As she passed the soldier, he tried to speak to her, but she ignored him.

With a heavy rumble, the train began to move again. They heard the passenger door at the back of the carriage slam shut. The blonde was back on board. Outside, Jack saw the soldier's panicked face. He began to run alongside the train, waving.

'Open the door!' Jack called to the young woman. 'The soldier's still outside.'

'I know,' the woman said, in a cold voice.

Jack felt a terrible fear deep in his stomach. He didn't know what was going on. He turned to Hannah. 'I don't like this,' he said.

'Both of you sit down,' the blonde woman commanded.

'What about the soldier?' Jack demanded.

'He's lucky,' the blonde said. 'He has a long walk back to his barracks, that's all.'

The train began to pick up speed. Jack could see the soldier now. He was running after the train, but without a hope of catching it.

'Both of you sit down,' the woman said again, reaching into her bag. 'Do as you're told, and nobody need get hurt.'

'What's going on?' Hannah asked. 'Why are you doing this?'

'No more questions,' the woman said, taking something out of the bag. 'From now on, you'll do exactly what I say or you'll answer to this!'

There was a gun in her hand.

Chapter Six
A Sticky Situation

'WHAT HAPPENED TO the old lady?' Jack asked.

The young woman laughed. 'That's none of your business. You two should be asleep, like the rest of them. It would be a lot easier for both of you.'

'I did fall asleep,' Hannah said, 'with a toffee in my mouth. I got so sleepy that it fell out before I'd eaten much of it.'

'That's a pity for you,' the blonde

woman said. 'Things would be a lot easier if you were both fast asleep. You should have had a hot drink, then you'd be out cold and I wouldn't have needed to get out my gun.'

'I've still got my toffee,' Hannah said, in a little girl voice, 'and Jack gave me his. I don't want to be awake. The gun frightens me. Would it be all right if we ate them now?'

Jack cursed. He didn't want to go to sleep. With the soldier gone, he and Hannah were the only ones who could save the other people on the train. The blonde woman smiled.

'Yes,' she said, her voice softening. 'That's a good idea. Go ahead and eat the sweets.'

Jack expected Hannah to ask him for the toffees she had passed to him earlier. Instead, she reached into her pocket and pulled out two different toffees.

'Eat it, Jack,' Hannah said.

Of course! He remembered, Hannah had been eating toffee earlier. She must still have some left. Jack tried to look unwilling.

'I don't know,' he said.

The blonde woman frowned. She was still pointing the gun at him. Reluctantly, he put the sweet into his mouth and started to chew.

'I'm not going until I've seen you swallow it all,' the blonde said.

Jack ate as fast as he could. Luckily, the toffee was softer than the one the old lady had given him, almost fudge-like. He managed to swallow it.

'Finished,' he muttered.

'Open your mouth!'

Jack did as he was told.

'Feel tired,' Hannah said. She rested her head on Jack's shoulder.

'Let me see inside your mouth as well. Come on, girl, open wide!'

Hannah gave a huge yawn, showing off her tonsils and empty mouth.

'I feel sleepy too,' Jack announced, and closed his eyes.

They both pretended to be fast asleep.

Soon, the blonde woman was whispering, but Jack could make out most of the words. Who was she talking to?

Jack risked opening his eyes. She was directly in front of him, talking to the young man on the right. As Jack watched, she lifted her head and turned back. Jack only just managed to close his eyes in time.

'All right, tiger,' she said, in an affectionate voice. 'They're out for the count.'

'Good thing too,' said a male voice which Jack recognized. It was the man with the short hair. 'Those kids are sharp,' he said. 'I heard them talking about the toffees before. They were on to us.'

'It doesn't matter, Craig. They'll be out for hours now. I guess they decided that it was better to fall asleep than to fall out of a train,' the woman said.

The bloke, Craig, laughed.

'Nice one, Brenda. You've played a blinder.'

'Let's see if I can find the keys.'

What keys? Jack wondered. Who were this Brenda and Craig? He heard a clanking noise and opened half an eye. Craig, the short-haired man in front of him, was standing up. An empty handcuff dangled from his wrist.

'You don't know what a relief it is not to be cuffed to that guard,' he told Brenda.

'And not to be going to prison,' she laughed.

'Is the boat waiting?'

'Hold on.' She looked in Jack's direction and he immediately closed his eye. 'I just want to make sure those kids are properly asleep.'

Craig laughed. 'My mother and her famous toffees,' he said. 'Did I tell you about the time when she …?'

'Sssh!' Brenda said. 'I'll just check his eyes.'

How did your eyes look when you were asleep? Jack wondered. Then he had a horrible feeling as Brenda pulled back his eyelids. He tried to stay calm, not allowing his eyes to focus. Then she let go.

'Yes, it looks like your mother's famous toffee did the trick.'

Jack heaved a sigh of relief.

So that was it, Jack thought. The old lady was Craig's mother. She had passed drugged sweets around while Brenda gave out drugged tea and coffee. They had missed the soldier because he stayed in the buffet until the last minute.

From the way they were talking, Brenda, the blonde woman with the gun, must be the prisoner's girlfriend or wife. And the balding man, the one whose head Jack had accidentally cut, must be a prison warder escorting Craig to the prison at Bragoon. Jack wondered what he was going to prison for.

'How long before we're there?' Craig asked Brenda.

'I'm not sure. Depends on whether the line's clear. It hasn't been used since they closed it down last year.'

There was a moaning noise.

'What's going on?' someone asked. It was the woman with the stud through her nose, the one who'd been locked in the toilet earlier. Brenda swore.

'Wait a minute,' Jack heard Craig whisper. 'She might go back to sleep.'

'Where am I?' asked the woman in a confused voice. Jack heard her standing up. 'Is *everyone* on this train asleep?' she asked, impatiently.

'Not quite everyone,' Brenda said in a forced voice. Jack heard her striding past him. 'Are you all right? You had a bit of a funny turn earlier.'

'Did I?' The young woman sounded confused.

'What are we going to do?' Hannah whispered to Jack.

'I don't know,' he hissed back.

'My mobile phone's in my bag. If we could get hold of it ...'

'But how?'

Her bag was on the luggage rack above their heads. They could hear Brenda speaking.

'When we get to Bragoon a doctor can look at you. Until then, why don't you go back to sleep?'

Brenda walked right past Hannah and Jack.

'It's all right,' Jack heard her tell Craig. 'She's back in the land of nod.'

'That stuff's meant to knock them out for hours,' Craig said.

'Maybe she didn't drink the whole cup,' Brenda said.

'What if the warder wakes up?' Craig asked.

'Don't worry. I gave him a double dose and he drank it all. I checked.'

The conversation continued, but the train got noisier and Jack couldn't make out all the words. Hannah poked his shoulder.

'If we get the phone,' she whispered, 'one of us could pretend to need the toilet and call the police from there.'

'Good idea,' Jack said. He was trying to sound encouraging, but didn't hold out much hope. How could they get their hands on the phone without being seen?

Chapter Seven
Lights Out

As the train hurtled on, Hannah listened to Craig and Brenda's conversation. A lot of it was lovey-dovey stuff. They had been engaged to be married until Craig got arrested. They seemed to be planning a new life abroad.

'Do you think the police are on to us yet?' Craig asked, at one point.

'Bound to be,' Brenda said. 'They'll have picked up the soldier.'

'Then won't they be waiting for us?'

Brenda laughed. 'The only way they'll get us is if they send another train.'

'What about a helicopter?' Craig asked.

'Scottish police don't have their own helicopter. They have to borrow one from Mountain Rescue and ...'

Before she could finish the sentence, something happened.

'What the ...?' Craig said.

'Don't worry,' Brenda said. 'It's only a tunnel.'

'Quick!' Hannah whispered to Jack. 'The phone!'

Hannah heard Jack stand on the seat. She heard the luggage rack rattle and hoped that Craig and Brenda hadn't heard it too. This was madness. The train would be out of the tunnel in a moment. Craig and Brenda would see that they were awake and take the phone.

But the tunnel must have been a long one. She heard Jack slide the bag under her seat and sit back down. Hannah began feeling for the phone.

'The tunnel's ending,' Jack whispered, just as she found it.

There was no time for Jack to put the bag back. Hannah closed it and pushed the bag under her seat. She felt Jack's head flop back against hers.

'Did you hear something then?' Craig asked Brenda.

'I'm not sure,' she said. 'Let's have a quick look around.'

Hannah slid the mobile phone inside her jeans pocket.

'Wish me luck,' she whispered to Jack. Then she started to moan.

Craig shouted, 'The girl's awake!'

Hannah had never done any acting, but she had to be convincing now. She stretched herself.

'Where am I?' she asked in an exaggeratedly sleepy voice.

'On a train,' said Brenda, trying to sound gentle. 'Go back to sleep, dear. We'll wake you up when we arrive.'

'Need the toilet,' Hannah moaned.

'I'm sure you can wait.'

'Need it now!' Hannah almost shouted, making herself sound like a six-year-old.

'All right,' Brenda said. 'I'll take you.'

'Give me your hand,' Hannah mumbled.

'My, you are sleepy, aren't you? Come

on now,' Brenda said, giving Hannah her hand. 'And I want you to leave the door open. We don't want you locking yourself in and falling asleep in there, do we?'

'Can't go with the door open!' Hannah said. 'People can see!'

'Oh, all right!' Brenda snapped. 'But don't you dare lock the door, or there'll be trouble.'

Hannah heard the door shut. She found the loo seat and sat down on it. Then she kicked out her legs so that the door couldn't be quickly opened. Next, she got out the phone and, feeling for the keys, switched it on. Finally, she began to dial. Nine. Nine. Nine.

Jack heard the toilet door open and close. He waited in agonizing suspense.

Brenda was standing by the toilet. Despite the engine noise, Brenda might be able to hear Hannah speaking to the police. How could Jack protect her?

'She's taking too long,' Craig called out. 'Open the door. Don't let her fall asleep again.'

'All right,' Brenda said.

Jack panicked. He had to think of something to distract them.

'Help!' he screamed.

'Stop that!' Craig said, in a rough voice.

'Help, help!' Jack called out. 'They're coming for me, help!'

'Shut up!' Craig said, putting a hand over Jack's mouth.

Jack heard Brenda coming back.

'What's going on?' she asked.

'The boy, he's …'

'He should be fast asleep,' Brenda interrupted. 'Unless ... look, his eyes are still shut. Take your hand off his mouth.'

'Monsters,' Jack muttered, then put on a begging voice. 'Save me from the monsters.'

'There, there,' Brenda said, putting a hand on Jack's shoulder. 'No monsters here. You're having a nightmare. Go back to sleep.'

But Jack made himself tremble and moan, insisting that he was surrounded by monsters. He only stopped when he heard the toilet flushing and Hannah calling for help.

'Your friend's having a nightmare,' Brenda told her. 'Can you calm him down?'

Hannah said 'tired'. Then she clamber- ed into her seat, rested her head on

Jack's shoulder, and pretended to sleep. As soon as he felt her next to him, Jack let his head lollop and pretended that he'd gone back to sleep too.

He desperately wanted to ask Hannah how she'd got on, but Brenda and Craig stayed close by them, watching. Jack could almost feel their breath on his face.

'I thought he was going to wake the others up,' Brenda said, after a while.

'I'd like to be able to get through this without killing anybody else,' Craig said.

What did he mean, Jack wondered, by 'anybody else'? Craig must be a murderer. He felt Hannah shiver. Then there was a loud creaking noise.

'What's happening?' Brenda asked. 'The train seems to be slowing down.'

'I'll look,' Craig said.

Jack heard him rush to the window.

Craig swore. 'Tree on the line. You stay here. I'll see if I can move it on my own.'

The train came to a halt. Jack heard Craig getting off the train. Brenda accompanied him down the corridor. When they were both out of earshot, Jack took his chance.

'Did you get through?' he asked Hannah.

'No. The signal wasn't strong enough. It must be because we're surrounded by hills.'

Jack tried not to let the disappointment sound in his voice.

'What do you think we should do now?' he asked Hannah. 'Take our chance and run for it?'

'You won't get far with me,' Hannah told him.

'Then what shall I do?' Jack asked,

urgently. 'We've got to do something.'

'You go if you like,' Hannah said.

'No. I can't desert you.'

Hannah gave him a brave smile.

Outside, they could hear Craig calling, 'I can't do this on my own!'

'I'm coming,' Brenda yelled and got off the train.

Jack risked a glimpse through the window. There was a big tree fifty metres down the line. Brenda and Craig would have their work cut out to move it. He told Hannah.

'What shall we do?' Hannah asked. 'Any ideas?'

'I'd like to know who's driving the train,' Jack said.

'They must have another accomplice,' Hannah told him.

He watched as the two hijackers

tried to move the tree. It seemed to be shifting slowly. 'I'm going to get out on the other side of the train,' he told Hannah. 'I'll see if I can find out what's going on.'

'Be careful,' Hannah said. 'I'll have another go at phoning the police.'

Jack hurried to the end of the corridor, passing the sleeping woman with the stud through her nose. He pulled down the window on the left-hand passenger door and got out without difficulty. Suppose the hijackers got back to the train before him? He might be stranded here in the middle of nowhere. But that was a risk he was going to have to take.

Thinking she was the only one awake, Hannah tried the phone again. It was still no good. Suddenly, someone tapped her shoulder. Hannah nearly screamed.

'Thank God someone else is awake!' a Scots accent said. 'I'm Katherine.'

It was the young woman who Jack had described as having a stud through her nose.

'I'm Hannah. Were you faking too?' Hannah asked.

'Just for the last few minutes,' Katherine said. 'When I woke up before, I worked out what was going on. After that I tried to force myself to stay awake, but I'm feeling pretty dreadful. I keep dropping off. You know who the bloke is, don't you?'

Hannah shook her head.

'He's Craig Costello, a convicted killer. I'm a reporter covering his case for the *Herald*. Craig's been in court because he injured another prisoner in Bragoon Prison. They added two years to his sentence. He's also part of the Costello clan. Craig's father and mother were behind the Scottish train robbery in the seventies. They were never caught. Rumour has it that they're in Bolivia. And Craig was convicted of ... blast!'

'What is it?' Hannah asked.

'They've managed to move the tree.'

'What are we going to do?'

'I don't know,' Katherine said. 'We'll think of something. Where's your friend?'

'Gone to find out who's driving. He should be back by now. Can you see him?'

'Sorry,' Katherine said. 'Would he have run off?'

'I don't think he's like that,' Hannah said.

'I hope he is,' Katherine said. 'Maybe he'll get help. Mind you, this place looks like the middle of nowhere. Uh-oh, Brenda's coming back. I'm going to my seat. I'll do my best to stay awake.'

Hannah inwardly cursed Jack. He'd promised to stay. Now it looked like he'd taken the first opportunity to run away. She didn't want to be stuck here without him. But at least Katherine was awake now.

What if Jack had been caught? What would Craig and Brenda do with him if they found him? Hannah heard the two hijackers getting back into the carriage.

The train began to move.

Chapter Eight
Last Chance

JACK RAN ALONGSIDE the carriage. He didn't know where the train had stopped. All he could see were faded green highlands, the grass scrubbed short by sheep. He didn't know what to do when he got to the front of the train either. Heart beating fast, he climbed on to the footplate and looked into the cramped driver's section. There, behind the seat, was a body.

Jack shivered. The body had to be the

train driver's. Was he dead? Cautiously, Jack turned the handle and opened the door. He got in, reached over and touched the man. His body was warm. Also, his hands were tied and he had a plaster across his mouth. He must be alive. Jack shook him.

'Mister, mister, wake up!'

But it was no good. He must have been drugged too. Who was driving the train? The new driver must be helping to move the tree. Should Jack risk a look?

As Jack edged his way past the driver's seat, the door on the left swung shut on him. Before Jack could look out of the right-hand door, he heard Craig's voice.

'That's far enough. We can get going now. Start her up again!'

Jack was scared. He had to get back to the carriage before the hijackers noticed he was gone. But he could hear the driver starting to open the door on the other side. He was trapped. He was bound to be caught.

What to do? The train driver was lying in the small area between the driver's seat and the door which connected it to the carriage. Jack crouched down beside him. Hopefully he wouldn't be visible to the new driver. There was no choice. He heard the door on the right close. At any moment, he might be discovered.

They began to move. Jack had left Hannah on her own. That was unforgivable. Craig and Brenda were bound to work out that if he was faking, so was Hannah. But there was nothing that he could do about it. He had to work out what was going on, then find a way to stop it.

Jack craned his neck to see who was driving the train. What he saw gave him a shock.

It was the little old lady.

Craig and Brenda's voices became louder which meant that they were getting nearer to Hannah. Any moment now, they would notice Jack's absence.

'That tree had moss on it,' Craig was saying. 'Must have been there for months. I thought you checked the whole line?'

'Not me personally,' Brenda told him. 'Anyway, we managed to move it.'

'Let's hope that there aren't any more obstacles like that.'

'The line's been closed for the best part of eighteen months,' Brenda pointed out. 'We're lucky they haven't bothered taking the track up.'

'I guess … hey, where's the boy?'

'With the blind girl.'

'No, he isn't,' Craig said, swearing. 'He was faking! I should have known he was faking.'

'Either that, or he's sleepwalked off the train,' Brenda said. 'Check the toilet.'

Moments later, Hannah heard Craig again. 'It's empty.'

'I think the girl's only pretending to be asleep,' Craig said when he'd returned.

'How can that be?' Brenda asked. 'We both watched her eat the toffee.'

'I don't know,' Craig replied. 'But we'll soon find out.'

Hannah felt a rough hand grip her shoulder.

'Time to wake up, Little Miss See-No-Evil,' Craig shouted. 'We want to know what's happened to your boyfriend.'

Hannah faked confusion. 'Where am I?'

'On a train,' Brenda said, comfortingly. 'Where's the boy?'

'What boy?' Hannah asked.

'The one you were sitting with.'

Hannah shook her head as though she didn't remember. 'I feel so tired,' she mumbled.

'Don't give me that!' Craig said. 'We want to know …'

'Leave her be,' Brenda interrupted. 'Whatever's happened to the boy, it doesn't matter. There's not far to go now.'

'We're running late,' Craig pointed out, anxiously. 'The train was late to begin with and we've just lost five minutes.'

'Four,' Brenda corrected him. 'Don't worry. It's within the margin of error.'

'How long will they wait?'

'Long enough.'

How long would *who* wait? Hannah wondered. And what would happen to the other passengers when they arrived? Would they be left to sleep off the knockout drops or would they all become hostages?

Maybe Katherine had a plan, but Hannah had no way of communicating with her. The situation didn't bear thinking about. Her only hope was that Jack was doing something to save them. Where was he?

Jack was beginning to get cramp in his right side. The train was so noisy that he could get away with moving about a little. But there wasn't much room to stretch in. Jack pressed his right foot against the side of the driver's compartment. The pressure eased the cramp a little.

As he pulled his foot back, it caught on something. Jack froze, but it was OK, the old lady hadn't noticed. What had his foot caught on? He twisted round. He struggled to reach round the driver's seat without giving himself away.

Yes! It was her carpet bag. Jack managed to pull the bag back. He didn't know what he was looking for, but rummaged around. There were some more toffees, tissues, a map and, most useful, a mobile phone. Jack took the map and the phone. It might be a way of keeping in touch with Hannah.

Suddenly, there was a massive rumble. They were braking again. Jack pushed the bag back and pressed up against the sleeping driver. If the old lady decided to open the connecting door into the carriage, he was sunk. The train shuddered to a stop. Jack had no way of telling if there was another obstacle or they had reached their destination.

He heard Craig's voice, but he couldn't hear what the prisoner was saying because the train door was closed. Then it opened. What if Craig saw Jack?

'We should have this moved in a

minute!' Craig called. 'Lock the carriage doors. We lost a lad last time we stopped. I don't want any of the other three getting out!'

Jack heard Brenda's voice. 'How far to go now?'

'Only a mile or so,' the old lady called back. 'We'll be at sea before you know it.'

'How many of the hostages do you think we should take with us?' Craig asked.

'One or two,' the old woman replied. 'The blind girl definitely. She's real protection. And the prison guard or the woman, whichever's least trouble.'

'And what do we do with them when we're safe away?'

The wicked old woman laughed. 'Dump them overboard, of course!'

Craig swore. 'This is harder than it looks. Give us a hand, would you?'

Yes! Jack thought. Now was his chance. He heard the old lady getting out of the train. The door swung shut behind her.

Keeping his head down, Jack squeezed round the left of the driver's seat, then risked a quick glance out of the window. The three hijackers were trying to shift some fencing which had fallen on to the line.

Jack had no idea how to drive the train, but somehow he had to get Hannah out before the hijackers used her as a hostage. If they hurried, there should be time. Squeezing past the sleeping driver, he tried to open the connecting door. He pushed with all his might.

At first he thought the door was jammed. Then, slowly, it opened and Jack charged through, shutting it behind him.

'It's me!' he called out. 'Hannah, are you all right?'

'I'm fine,' she said, still in the seat where he had left her. 'Where were you?'

Rapidly, Jack told her what had happened. He was surprised to find that the woman with the stud through her nose was awake too.

'This is Katherine,' Hannah told him. 'She's a reporter. Craig's an escaped prisoner, a murderer. The old lady is his mother.'

'And she's the one driving the train,' Jack said. 'Any other explanations can wait. Craig and Brenda will be back in a minute. You don't know how to drive a train, do you?' The question was to Katherine.

'I'm afraid not,' she said.

'Then let's try and escape through the front. The doors aren't locked.'

'Too late!' said Katherine, who was looking out of the window. 'They're coming!'

'I'll hide in the toilet,' Jack said. 'We'll think of something. Pretend to sleep. But be really careful when we stop. They mean to use you two as hostages!'

He shut himself in the toilet. He hadn't told Hannah and Katherine the worst bit – what the kidnappers would do to their hostages once they weren't needed any more. There was no point in scaring them more than they were scared already. But he had to find a way to stop it happening.

He heard the click of the doors unlocking. Craig and Brenda got back on. Once they'd gone past him, Jack reached into his pocket. He pulled out the map he'd taken from the old lady's bag. He didn't know where they were, so it wasn't much use. The map covered a hundred square miles, most of them coastline. There was no 'X' to mark the spot where they were heading.

Jack wished he'd paid more attention when they had done map-reading in the Scouts. What was the symbol for a disused railway line? He gave up on that and got out the mobile phone. It was expensive-looking and newer than Hannah's. Would it have a stronger signal?

The buttons were confusing. Jack had to wait for the train to start before risking making a noise. Then, as the carriage began to move, he figured out how to switch the phone on. Heart beating fast, he dialled three nines and listened. There was a short delay. Would it, could it work?

Somewhere, a phone began to ring.

Chapter Nine
The End of the Line

THE TRAIN SEEMED to be slowing down. Hannah listened to what was going on. Craig and Brenda were trying to decide which other person to take as a hostage. If only she'd given Jack her phone, she thought.

'Well, look at this!' she heard Craig say. 'See what I've found in this woman's handbag. She's a reporter. And for the *Herald* no less. Wake up, lassie!' His voice was menacing, horrible.

Hannah trembled as Craig ranted at Katherine. 'Why did your paper say all those things about me? Do you think they were true?'

'I don't know,' Katherine replied. She sounded petrified.

'Then I'll tell you,' Craig boasted. 'They were true. Every word. They were going to throw away the key this time. But instead, I'm the one with the key.'

'Wh-what do you mean?' Katherine asked, breathlessly.

'Put your hands behind your back.'

'Why?'

'You'll find out.'

Hannah heard a rattle, followed by a click. Craig had put one of his handcuffs on her. Hannah had been counting on Katherine, but the reporter would be unable to help her any more. Jack was their only hope.

She heard Craig dragging Katherine towards her. Then Hannah felt something cold and metallic on her wrist. She and Katherine were being handcuffed together.

'That'll slow you down,' Craig said.

'Now let's look through the rest of your bag,' Craig said, taunting Katherine. 'What's this? Some kind of miniature camera. What were you going to take a picture of?'

'N-nothing,' Katherine said. 'I always carry it with me.'

'*Don't believe you*,' Craig said in a sing-song, teasing voice. 'You wanted to take a photograph of the famous killer, Craig Costello, going into prison for the very last time. That was it, wasn't it?'

'Yes,' Katherine said. 'All right, yes. But like I said, I'm only doing my job.'

'And I was only doing mine,' Craig told her. 'If it wasn't for busybodies like you, I might still be doing it now. I've a good mind to …'

'This is it!' Brenda called, interrupting him. 'We're here!'

Hiding in the toilet, Jack finished explaining the situation to a police officer. Detective Sergeant Hunter told Jack that the police already knew about the runaway train.

'Craig Costello's a very dangerous man,' DS Hunter said. 'Be extremely careful.'

'Hold on,' Jack said.

He could hear the train braking.

'Are you still there?' DS Hunter asked.

Jack told him that he was. 'We haven't got that much time! The train's stopping again. Hopefully, they don't know I'm here. I might be able to sneak off the train after they've gone.'

'Maybe,' the DS said, 'but they'll probably have an accomplice or two waiting to meet the train. Take no chances.'

'Will you be able to get here in time?' Jack asked the DS.

'It depends where *here* is. I've got a map in front of me. I want you to look at yours.'

Jack got his map out.

'Now,' the DS said, 'can you find Clanark?'

'Yes.'

'And the train line?'

'What does it look like?'

'It's a black line with short thin lines across every centimetre.'

'Got it.'

'All right,' the DS said. 'Now, just above Clanark, the line splits into two. Follow the left-hand line for five centimetres. You should be at the coast.'

'I am, but there are no stations.'

'I know,' the DS said. 'Our guess is that they won't use a station. They'll have somebody meeting them with a boat. At the point where the train line's nearest to the coast, they'll stop the train and get out. There are a couple of bays which have no road access at all. The only way we can get to them is by helicopter or by sea.

'Now, I'm going to alert the coastguard and we're trying to locate Mountain Rescue's helicopter. We can borrow it if it's not in use. Don't worry, we're going to get to you. Now, describe what you can see from the window.'

'I can't see much at all,' Jack said. 'It's not a proper window and it doesn't open.'

He stared through the misted plastic. 'It's hazy. All I can see is an embankment.'

The train's engine was turned off. He could hear movement. Suddenly, Jack had to whisper. He explained that he couldn't see anything else.

'Never mind,' the DS said. 'We might be able to track you using the signal from your phone. Check how strong the batteries are.'

The battery symbol on the phone's LCD was three-quarters filled. Jack told the DS this.

'You should be good for at least an hour. I want you to leave the phone switched on so that we can trace you. If you get disconnected, call this number ...'

Jack memorized it.

Suddenly, he heard a train door being opened.

'I've got to go,' he whispered. 'They're on the move.'

'All right. We should be able to trace you with the phone in your pocket. But Jack, be very, very careful. Only follow them if you're sure that you can't be seen. The rest is up to us. We'll get there as soon as we can.'

Jack was on his own again. It was all very well for the police to tell him to be careful, but they weren't here. And they might not get here in time. If the kidnappers' plan went to schedule, it would be too late for Hannah and Katherine. Shivering with fear, he opened the toilet door. There was no noise at all. He stepped into the empty aisle and looked back at the carriage. Then he spoke into the phone.

'They've left the prison warder behind. He's still asleep. I'm going to get off the train now, see if I can find out where they've gone.'

Jack put the phone back into his pocket, then opened his suitcase. He took out his green cagoule. It would protect him from the weather and make him harder to spot. Quickly, he put it on, then got out of the train. A stiff sea breeze blew around him.

Jack scrambled up the embankment and looked around. Five figures were walking on a rough track not far from him. Ahead of them was a large hill. To each side of the track there was long grass and plenty of trees. He should be able to keep under cover.

Jack pulled his hood up, put his head down and began to follow.

Chapter Ten
The Sea

'FASTER!' BRENDA URGED Hannah and Katherine.

'Can't go any faster,' Hannah complained.

The ground was bumpy and slippery. She had already stumbled once, almost twisting her ankle. Was Jack following them? Hannah had no way of knowing.

'Watch out,' Katherine said. 'Steep bit ahead.'

They clambered up a rock path.

Twice, Hannah fell. The second time Katherine apologized, 'I'm not a lot of use.'

She sounded even more scared than Hannah. Craig had a grudge against Katherine, Hannah knew. She had good reason to be afraid.

Suddenly, the ground flattened out.

'We're on a cliff,' Katherine told Hannah. 'Beneath us is the sea.'

Jack was on open ground. He kept a good distance behind the five walkers. The sky was overcast and threatening rain, so the light wasn't good. Even so, one of them might turn and spot him at any moment. He needed to stay out of gunshot range.

There was a hill ahead. Jack couldn't see over it. Once the five got to the top, they vanished. Now Jack could run. He hurried until the path became steep, then clambered up the hill. When he got to the top, however, he stopped.

Jack was completely exposed. Beneath him, the five were climbing down a steep cliff. Their path was narrowly carved into its side. Hannah might overbalance at any moment, taking Katherine with her. At the bottom of the cliff was a tiny, concealed cove.

Jack lay on the ground, looking. The five were walking at a fair pace with the old lady leading the way. He could follow them down. The fugitives were unlikely to look back until they reached the bottom. But then he would be a sitting duck.

Jack noticed something else. At the edge of the cove was a small jetty. An open boat was sailing towards it, a twenty-footer with an engine. The sea was rough, so the boat's passage was slow, but it would dock in a couple of minutes. Jack was going to be too late. So were the police. Once they were safely away, the Costellos would throw Hannah and Katherine overboard. There was no time. Jack got out the old lady's mobile phone and spoke into it.

'They're nearly there!' he told the detective sergeant. 'You've got to hurry!'

The climb down the cliff face was terrifying. Hannah had never done anything more dangerous in her life. She could feel Katherine shivering and shaking. A heavy wind blew, freezing

Hannah to her bones. Then it began to rain.

'We're at the bottom,' Katherine said, 'but watch out, there's seaweed on the stones.'

Sure enough, Hannah went over. Katherine tumbled on top of her. Craig swore.

'Help those two up,' he told Brenda.

'Take your time,' Katherine whispered in Hannah's ear. 'I think I see something.'

Hannah didn't have to act. Getting up was difficult.

'Can't you take these handcuffs off?' Katherine asked. 'There's nowhere for us to run after all.'

Craig only laughed. Now Hannah could hear what Katherine had seen. It was a distant engine. The Costellos were wrong about the police not having a helicopter. But once they were all on the boat, how could a helicopter rescue them?

The rain grew heavier. Hannah was helped back to her feet. How long before the Costellos noticed the helicopter? If she and Katherine could only slow them down ... but now they were being dragged along again. Hannah felt sand beneath her feet.

There was a sudden noise from Hannah's coat. For a moment, she didn't know what it was. But Brenda did. It was her phone ringing.

'How long have you had that?' Brenda asked as Hannah stopped and took the phone out of her inside pocket.

'All the time,' she said, calmly

switching the phone to 'talk' before Brenda or Craig could intervene. There was a policeman at the other end. How, she wondered, had he got this number? Hannah spoke to him for a moment. Then she called to Craig.

'It's for you.'

Jack couldn't stop himself. The rain was so thick now that visibility was poor. Also, the people on the beach were distracted by the phone. They were unlikely to notice him. So he hurried down the steep, narrow path. The helicopter noise was getting nearer, but Jack could no longer see what was happening below. His main worry was being spotted by whoever was on the boat. But it was too late to turn back. He scurried as fast as he could along the narrow ledge which led down to the sea.

Hannah could hear both sides of the phone conversation. The detective told Craig that they'd go easy on him if he let the hostages go.

'I'm in charge here,' Craig replied, laughing.

'How did they get this number?' Brenda hissed to Hannah.

'I gave it to Jack,' she said. No point in lying.

'But you've still got the phone,' Brenda said, confused, 'so how could he …?'

'Call the boat on your mobile,' Craig told his mother, covering the receiver. 'Ask what's holding him up.'

'My phone's gone!' the old lady said after a moment. 'Where the …?'

'What's that noise?' Brenda said, interrupting her. 'Get off the phone, Craig! They're only trying to distract us. Look over there! It's a helicopter!'

Jack was nearly at the bottom of the cliff when he saw the boat turn back. The pilot must have seen the helicopter and decided to run for it. Craig was standing ahead of him, facing away. He had a gun in one hand and Hannah's phone in the other. Craig was swearing at the police, saying that he'd kill both hostages unless they let him get away in their helicopter. The police would never let him leave, Jack knew that. He had already warned the detective that Craig planned to kill his hostages.

Everyone was watching the helicopter come lower. It would be very dangerous for it to land. The tide was on its way in, so the beach was very narrow. Craig was waving the gun, pointing it at the helicopter. The convict was no longer speaking into the phone, Jack saw. He picked up the biggest rock he could find, then dialled Hannah's number.

The helicopter was deafening. Help was so near, yet so far. Beneath the noise from the helicopter, Hannah heard her phone ring again. Craig swore.

'Answer it,' Brenda yelled. 'They might have a deal to offer.'

'Don't want a deal,' Craig said, then there was a sudden thud.

'Jack!' Katherine exclaimed. 'Quick, Hannah, help me get on top of him!'

And Hannah felt herself being pulled to the ground.

'Hit him!' Katherine urged, confusing Hannah. Who was she meant to hit? Hannah flung her arms around.

'Not me!' Katherine called out. 'Him!'

Jack's stone had caught Craig on the side of the head. The killer went down, dropping both the phone and the gun. As Jack ran towards them, Katherine and Hannah jumped on to the escaped murderer. Hannah was going wild, arms flailing everywhere. From the helicopter, a voice spoke through a loudhailer.

'Armed police! Surrender and you will come to no harm.'

Jack got to the mass of bodies just as Brenda noticed him. The gun was on the sand. Brenda started to reach for it, but there was a warning shot from the helicopter. She hesitated, allowing time for Jack to snatch the gun. He threw it into the sea as the helicopter began to land. Police officers chased across the sand towards them.

'It's all right,' Jack called to Hannah and Katherine. 'We're safe!'

As Jack spoke, Craig scrambled free of Hannah and Katherine. But there was nowhere for him to run to. Within moments, the police had all three hijackers handcuffed. While they were doing this, Jack searched Ma Costello's bag. He found what he was looking for. Triumphantly, he got out the keys to the handcuffs.

Once Jack had freed Hannah and Katherine, Hannah reached out her arm, feeling for him. Then all three of them hugged.

'I didn't think that we were going to get out of that,' the reporter said.

'Next time I run away,' Jack said, 'I'll hitch-hike or go by plane.'

'Don't be daft,' Hannah told him as Craig, Brenda and Ma Costello were led away. 'You meet much more interesting people on a train.'

Mad Myths: Must Fly!

by Steve Barlow & Steve Skidmore

**Crazy kids, barmy teachers and a mad myth
or two!**

Disaster hits the school trip when Perce and Andy
rescue a shipwrecked sailor and discover that knowing
the wrong person could get them blown away.

DISCOVER . . .

SURFERS

. . . FAST PACY READS

Mutiny in Space

by Cherith Baldry

Red Alert

Cadets Jake Fraser and Ellie Carr are determined to
overthrow Lt. Quentin when he and half the crew of
the Venture mutiny. But the situation becomes doubly
difficult as it seems that Quentin is not the only one
who wants control of the ship . . .

DISCOVER . . .

SURFERS

. . . FAST PACY READS
